W9-BVM-257

ATTACK OF THE EVIL MINIONS!

By Kirsten Mayer • Illustrated by Ed Miller

Based on the Motion Picture Screenplay
Written by Cinco Paul & Ken Daurio

L B

Little, Brown and Company   New York Boston

See that guy there among all the yellow fellows? That's Gru. He was once a villain, but now he has turned the secret lab under his house into a jelly factory! The yellow fellows are Minions. See all the Minions at work making jelly? Well, most of them are working.

Quiet, please—testing in progress.

"Tell me when testing.
1...2...3...Oops!"

The bad news is that the jelly tastes gross.
Kevin asks Gru, "Boss! Topah-leena-la belly?"
Gru throws his hands up in the air.
"You know what?" he says. "Let's shut it down. We are
officially out of the jelly business!"

Later that night, the doorbell rings at Gru's house. . . .

DING-DONG!

Oh no! A mysterious villain grabs the Minion! So many Minions, so little time.

Meanwhile, the other Minions are hanging out. It's good to be a Minion!

"Hey! Jerry, Kevin, keep an eye on things, okay?" asks Gru. "I'm going out."

The Minions take a look around the house. All is quiet, so they decide to have some fun.

Kevin nudges Jerry. "Hey, putt-putt?" he asks.

Jerry giggles. "Oh! Ha, ha, ha!"

The Minions tiptoe outside, looking for a burglar. "Boca? Boca?" they wonder.

Suddenly, a stray cat jumps out of a garbage can.

CLANG!

Kevin and Jerry laugh at each other for being so scared.

"Looka, too!" They point at each other.

The pointing turns into a wrestling match, but they freeze when a strange beam of light shines down from above. . . .

Two more Minions missing!

The next day, an ice cream truck drives by the house!

RING-A-LING!

Gru should really mind his Minions—someone keeps taking them!

Someone has collected mucho Minions and put them on a beach. They don't know it, but the Minions are trapped! What will happen to them? A Minion is a terrible thing to waste.

"Bello!" says Kevin.

"Compai!" says Tom.

In another secret lab, the villain has plans for the Minions! The Minions don't notice the purple goo.

What will that purple goo do to them?

"BLAAAH..."

It turns Tom into a monster!
Yellow is no longer mellow.

The new Evil Minions are unstoppable.

Flames don't burn them. Explosives are just a mild tummy ache. And they eat metal…lots of metal.

The mastermind behind the Minion mania is known as El Macho!

"The time has come, my purple army!" he cries. "I will unleash you, and you will eat the entire city! The world will be ours!"

El Macho looks around. "Hey! Minions, what are you doing? Pay attention! Stop eating the rocket! We need that! Get a hold of your brains! Everybody, back in line!"

El Macho unleashes his Evil Minions onto the world.
First stop: Gru's house. It's an attack of the Evil Minions!

Purple Evil Minions eat through the walls of Gru's lab! The Minions don't know what to do! What should they do?

One Minion throws a leftover jar of jelly at the purple monsters.

The jelly is a cure!
The monster turns
back into Kevin!

"GULP!"

Gru assembles his Minions—now he knows
what to do. He points to a vat of unused jelly
and says, "Team Minion, all hands on deck!
Let's put this horrible jelly to good use!"

"*Eye, eye*, captain!" they shout.

The Minions load globs of jelly onto a blaster ship and zoom into the air to zap all the Evil Minions with splats of sticky stuff.

"It's over, El Macho! You lose!" yells Gru in triumph as Minions swarm the villain.

"Noooooo!" cries El Macho. "My Minions!"

"*My* Minions," says Gru. "The best Minions ever!"